Jirohattan

by HANA MORI

Translated by
Tamiko Kurosaki
and
Elizabeth Crowe

Illustrated by
Elizabeth Crowe

Bess Press
P. O. Box 22388
Honolulu, Hawaii 96823

Acknowledgment

The co-translators would like to thank Chris Crowe for his invaluable assistance and support in translating and refining the English version of *Jirohattan*.

Cover art: Elizabeth Crowe
Cover design: Paula Newcomb

Jirohattan by Hana Mori
Copyright © 1975 by Hatsue Nakamura
English translation rights arranged with
Alice-kan Publishing Co., Ltd., Tokyo
through Japan Foreign-Rights Centre

English translation copyright © 1993
by Tamiko Kurosaki and Elizabeth Crowe

Library of Congress
Catalog Card Number: 93-72833

ISBN: 0-880188-69-4

Table of Contents

"Hiroki," called the grandmother, "come and
sit here by me. When I visit this cemetery I
always sit on these steps to rest."

CHAPTER 1

ะ๛๛

The Bell Tower

Deep in the rolling mountains of Japan, a young boy and his grandmother climbed a set of roughly hewn stone steps leading to a cemetery and farther up, a bell tower.

"Hiroki," called the grandmother, "come and sit here by me. When I visit this cemetery I always sit on these steps to rest." The old woman adjusted her gray kimono and lowered herself gently onto the step leading up to the bell tower. "Usually I come here alone, but I'm glad that you are with me today.

"Come, sit next to me. We can see the whole village from here. The river that runs behind the village is the Okawa River." The grandmother pointed and the little boy leaned forward to see. "It flows into the Maruyama River and from there goes all the way to the Sea of Japan.

"The bridge over the river is the Itoya Bridge. And there beyond the bridge we can see a long building on the mountainside. That's the village grade school.

"Listen! A bush warbler is singing. Spring has come to Tajima.

"Being here reminds me of a boy I once knew named Jirohattan."

"Jirohattan?" asked Hiroki. "Wasn't he the funny boy who always said, 'It's three an' five, five, five, five o'clock,' whenever he was asked the time?"

"That's right. You have a good memory. These stone steps were Jirohattan's favorite place. He used to sit on the very step you're sitting on now with his eyes half closed and watch the clouds. Whenever I'm here, I feel like he is sitting here too." She closed her eyes for a moment and remembered.

"Today," she smiled, "I'll tell you the story of Jirohattan. I'll start with the first time I met him."

⋰⋰⋰⋰

It was spring in the year 1928. I had just graduated from Akashi Women's College as an elementary school teacher and asked to be assigned to a small village school. They sent me to the school you're looking at now.

I took a train from Akashi to Yabu, a small and isolated station. Everything looked strange and I got off the train feeling lonely and a little afraid.

Several women at the station greeted me warmly, "Hello."

"Nice weather we're having, isn't it?"

It made me feel better that the people were friendly even though I was a stranger to their little village.

An old janitor from the school met me. He loaded my belongings onto a handcart. All I had was a desk, a bookcase and books, my bedding and a wicker trunk filled with my clothing.

"We've got a long, rough trip to make," said the kind old man. "Will you be all right?"

"Don't worry, I love walking," I said cheerfully and followed behind him while he pulled the cart up the road.

Soon we were out of the village. A crystal clear stream ran by the road, and bright yellow dandelions raised their heads along its sides. Mountains closed in on both sides of the path. It looked as if we were entering an endless green tunnel. I started to feel sad again as I plodded along behind the cart but tried to cheer up by reminding myself that I had wanted to come here.

After some time, we met a boy walking clumsily along the road. His roughly cut black hair hung over his forehead, and he seemed to be concentrating very hard on crossing a dirt bridge.

"Uncle!" called the boy with a cockeyed grin.

"Oh, Jirohattan," answered the janitor.

"Uncle, let _me_ pull it!" The boy ran up and quickly slipped in between the cart's poles.

"This is Jirohattan," said the janitor. "He's twelve or thirteen, but his body has grown much faster than his mind." The janitor tapped his forehead and smiled at me.

"Pull it with care, Jirohattan. Teacher's belongings are on it." The janitor and I followed behind the cart, talking. Suddenly the cart stopped and flipped backward with the empty poles sticking up.

"Jirohattan, what's wrong?" The janitor ran to him.

"My shoe is off." Jirohattan sat under the poles, slipping his straw sandal's strap between his toes. The janitor and I watched him with a laugh. Then we heard the splash. My wicker trunk had fallen into the water! The ropes must have loosened while the cart was tipped up. The janitor dashed into the stream and brought out my dripping trunk. It was soaked! And in it were my best silk kimonos.

At last we arrived at the house where I was going to live.

"What a wicked welcome!" clucked the landlady as she set out rods at the wide gateway to hang up my wet kimonos.

Like all young women's kimonos, mine were lined with red silk. As I hung my kimonos on the rods, the red dye from the lining quickly spread to the outside of the wet kimonos and trickled onto the ground.

"I'm sorry, terribly sorry. I hope they're not ruined. If only I had been pulling the cart . . ." The janitor kept bowing to me.

"You should have known better than to let Jirohattan pull the cart," the landlady scolded while the janitor continued to apologize. Jirohattan cocked his eyes at the red drips and, like a turtle, tucked his head into his shoulders.

As I watched the red dye trickle on the dry

4

Then we heard the splash. My wicker
trunk had fallen into the water!

earth and spread into growing dark crimson puddles, the whole situation seemed funny and I chuckled. Then Jirohattan started to laugh.

"Shame, Jirohattan!" said the janitor with a frown. "You shouldn't laugh when you've ruined all the kimonos Teacher brought. Why don't you apologize?"

"Would all your kimonos grow red spots if they got wet?" Jirohattan asked me with a wondering look.

Then all three of us, the janitor, landlady and I, couldn't help but laugh.

That was the beginning of my friendship with Jirohattan.

❧❧❧

CHAPTER 2

The Picture Book

"Look down there." The grandmother turned and pointed to another part of the valley. "Do you see the field that is so green? It's filled with milkweed. Soon it will blossom into a beautiful field of wildflowers.

"Even as a young man in his twenties, Jirohattan still loved to play tag and sumo with the village children there. It was a wonderful place to play. When your father was small, he used to play there too."

❧❧❧

"Hey! Come on! Let's play tag!" called out Kin, who was the oldest boy. Jirohattan and the children ran across the green carpet of milkweed to gather around him.

"Paper, Rock, Scissors!" yelled the children to determine who would be "it."

Jirohattan held out an open hand, paper. The

children all held out scissors. They knew that Jirohattan always held out paper. They would watch Kin to see what he would do. If he did scissors, all the children would be scissors too. If he held out his fist, rock, all the children held out rock.

Since Kin held out scissors today, the others were scissors too. So as always, Jirohattan was "it." He chased the children, running awkwardly with both arms flung out wide, tottering as if he were pushed by the wind.

"Jirohattan, catch me!" called out one boy. Jirohattan chased after him.

"Over here! Get me!" yelled another and Jirohattan turned and took off after that boy.

Soon, as had been agreed beforehand, one of the children would fall down. Today it was the smallest child's, Sei's, turn. Sei ran to Jirohattan.

"Jirohattan!" he called and fell down.

Jirohattan laughed aloud and jumped on Sei. "I got him! I got him!"

All the children dashed up and piled onto Jirohattan.

"I can't breathe," squealed Sei.

The children rolled off the pile and lay down on the milkweed. Breathing hard, Jirohattan put both hands beneath his head and looked up at the sky.

"How old are you, Jirohattan?" asked Yachan.

Jirohattan grinned. "Don't know."

"Of course you do," said Sabu. He jerked Jirohattan's hand.

"I don't," he pouted.

Then the children piled on Jirohattan, hitting his legs and tickling him all over.

Jirohattan squirmed and laughed. His long face became square, scrunched up into giggles.

"Help me up!" pleaded Jirohattan. The children pulled him up by his arms.

"How old are you, Jirohattan?" all the children asked in chorus.

"Same as neighbor Shinyan," replied Jirohattan.

"How old is Shinyan then?"

"He was born in the year of the monkey."

"Then how old are you?"

"Same as Shinyan."

"How old is Shinyan?"

"Born in the year of the monkey."

"So, how old are you?"

"Same as Shinyan."

And so it went, on and on, faster and faster until Jirohattan and the children ended it by bursting into a roar of laughter.

The spring wind carried the happy sound across the meadow to the surrounding mountains.

"Jirohattan, will we have good weather tomorrow?" the children would often ask. Then they gathered to peer under Jirohattan's nose.

"According to Jirohattan's weather forecast, tomorrow will be a fine day!" one of the children exclaimed.

"Jirohattan's nose is dry," the children announced one after another. Jirohattan quickly wiped his nose and beamed.

When Jirohattan had a runny nose, it would rain the following day. But when his nose was dry, the next day would be clear. Jirohattan's nose was more accurate than the weather forecast on the radio. It was one of the wonders of the village.

In Tajima it rains so often that we have a saying, "Though you forget your lunch box, remember your umbrella!"

The children would go and see Jirohattan's nose the day before an athletic event or a field trip. Adults also found his weather predictions useful. Jirohattan's nickname became "Weather Forecaster."

ra;ra;ra

"Hiroki," said the grandmother, "have you learned about World War II at school? Well, when Jirohattan was twenty-eight or twenty-nine, his mother worked as a telegraph messenger with the post office in town.

"A woman as a telegraph messenger?" marveled Hiroki.

"Does that seem strange to you? Many men were enlisted in the army during the war and there was a shortage of workers. Women had to take the place of men and work very hard.

"The village is about three and a half miles from town. Jirohattan's mother used to go to work on her late husband's old bicycle."

ra;ra;ra

"She's coming!" Yachan shouted. Jirohattan's mother was back from work, pushing the old bicycle up the steep road.

"Mama!"

"Mama!"

The children called to her as if she were their own mother. She sometimes brought back old books or magazines for them. During the war, one could not afford new books. Even old magazines were difficult to get. So the children were eager for anything to read.

They waited anxiously to see if Jirohattan's mother would bring them a book.

"Come! I've got a book for you!" she said.

The children's eyes glowed as they watched her open her bag.

"Look!"

Jirohattan's mother pulled out a picture book titled *The Tales of Taro Urashima*. All the children cheered with delight.

She explained that she had gotten the book from Mrs. Takemura, who had come to the neighboring village as an evacuee from Osaka. Jirohattan's mother had gone to deliver a telegram to Mrs. Takemura and had met her six-year-old son, who was ill.

"How I wish my son could have some rice soup, just a little each meal," Mrs Takemura said weeping.

Jirohattan's mother saw the boy's very thin hand sticking out from beneath his bed quilt and felt sorry for him. The next day she brought Mrs. Takemura some rice from her small garden.

"I'll be glad to pay for the rice," said Mrs. Takemura. But Jirohattan's mother refused.

"Take something!" urged Mrs. Takemura.

"Don't worry about it. I'm happy to help your boy," Jirohattan's mother said and started to leave.

Then she saw the picture book lying on the porch and asked for it.

In those days, except for farming families, no one could get any rice, even if they lived in the country. All necessities were rationed, including food. The only food available through rations was a bit of ground corn or wheat chaff. We used that to make dumpling soup.

Black-marketeers came along, buying large amounts of rice at a high price from farmers and selling it on the black market for a huge profit. The farmers who had stored rice or sold it to the black-marketeers refused to sell rice to either evacuees or villagers who were crying from hunger.

Mrs. Takemura had asked neighboring farmers to sell her some rice for her sick son, but she could not get even a handful from them.

But back to the picture book . . .

"Here, Kin, read it to the others." Jirohattan's mother handed the book to Kin, who was a good reader.

The children sat in a circle on the milkweed blossoms with Kin in the center.

"Once upon a time, in a seaside village, there lived a fisherman whose name was Taro Urashima. One day Taro came across a poor turtle that was being hurt by some children. He felt sorry for the turtle . . ."

Jirohattan sat among the children and listened

The children sat in a circle on the milkweed
blossoms with Kin in the center.

to the story, tugging on the few hairs that sprouted from his chin. The story told of a palace under the sea where Taro was taken by the turtle he had saved.

In the book was a picture of the sea princess at the palace. "Wait!" Jirohattan patted Kin's hand and gazed at the picture. "She is beautiful! Hohohoo, hohohoo!" Jirohattan beamed. How he loved the picture of the princess!

In the past, Jirohattan always gave the children the book after it had been read, and the children had already decided whose turn it was to keep this book.

But today Jirohattan said, "This one is mine," and he tucked the book tightly under his arm.

"Give it here! It's my turn to have it!" yelled Yachan. "Give it to me, give it to me!" Yachan jumped on Jirohattan.

"No! It's mine!" said Jirohattan and off he ran, carrying Yachan on his back.

The other children ran after them, Jirohattan running away with the book and Yachan clutching onto his back, shouting, "I want that book. Give it to me, give it to me!"

ɛɜʑɛɜʑ

A Red Letter

"In May 1943, Jirohattan's closest friend, Shinyan, received a red letter.

"We called draft notices red letters. Do you know what a draft notice is? If you get this notice, you have to enlist in the army by the date stated on the paper. At that time, a great many young men in the village had been called into the armed forces. In those days, getting a red letter and enlisting in the army was considered a most honorable event."

ɛɜʑɛɜʑ

The day Shinyan got his red letter, the blue sky stretched clear and bright. That was rare in Tajima.

Children's Day is in May. I tried to make the traditional rice cakes with a little bit of corn flour and had brought back some *sankira* leaves from the mountain to use for the wrappings.

Then Grandma Okane came to see me. If there was any news that all the villagers should know, it was Grandma Okane's job to tell it from house to house. "Teacher," Grandma Okane called to me. I was no longer teaching, but all the villagers continued to call me Teacher. "Shinyan finally got his red letter. He's leaving tomorrow morning."

"Tomorrow morning," I echoed sadly.

"The farewell party will be given tonight," she said.

Just then, Jirohattan came up with his arms full of *itadori* shoots. *Itadori* is a wild grass. When we couldn't get pickles, we ate *itadori* by peeling off the skin, slicing and flavoring it with vinegar or salt.

"Here, Teacher," he said as he offered me his armful.

"Been in the mountains again?" asked Grandma Okane.

"Uh huh," Jirohattan answered. "Do you want some?"

"No, not me. Give them all to Teacher," she said and then looked straight at him. "Jirohattan, Shinyan got his red letter." She patted his back as she told him.

"Oh," Jirohattan said, looking first at Grandma Okane and then at me. He took one of the *itadori* shoots, peeled off its skin and bit it with a loud crunch.

"He doesn't understand, I suppose," said Grandma Okane. "Jirohattan, let Teacher explain it to you." Then she turned and left.

"Jirohattan," I tried to explain, "Shinyan will go

16

to battle for our country. We will miss him, but we'll look forward to when he comes back." Jirohattan didn't pay any attention to what I was saying, but just kept on crunching on the *itadori*.

That night a farewell party was given for Shinyan.

The school principal, a policeman from the substation, the mayor and many others from the village gathered to honor Shinyan. Because it was an army enlistment celebration, there was a special supply of rationed food. Everyone was having a great time, drinking *sake*, singing war songs, and shouting many cheers of *banzai* for Shinyan.

Jirohattan was leaning against a sooty wooden pillar in the kitchen, watching the people celebrate.

"Jirohattan, you are lucky . . ." Shinyan's mother said and sobbed. Jirohattan looked puzzled and cocked his head to the side. "Jirohattan, why don't you go out and talk with Shinyan?" I suggested. Grinning, he went up to Shinyan.

"Jirohattan, I'm going to battle," said Shinyan, taking Jirohattan's hands and clasping them tightly. "Be well, my friend, I wish you well."

Jirohattan had always gone everywhere with Shinyan. So the children had made up a song that went like this:

When you want to find Shinyan, look for Jirohattan.
When you want to find Jirohattan, look for Shinyan.

Jirohattan's father had been a highly respected plasterer, and Shinyan was his apprentice. Jirohattan's father would boast about his apprentice, "I'll make Shinyan into a fine plasterer who someday will plaster the walls at the Emperor's palace."

And about Jirohattan, he would say, "My Jirohachi is slow-witted, but when he learns something, he stays with it. His flat feet are just right for mixing the wall mud and he is big, perfect for a plasterer's son. I'll train him to be a good helper for Shinyan."

Wherever Jirohattan's father and Shinyan worked, Jirohattan went with them to mix the wall mud. He would roll up his trousers and, splashed with mud, stamp patiently on the mixture of red clay and chopped straw. If not told to stop, he would continue to stamp from morning to night.

Jirohattan's father was a cheerful, hard-working man. But he became ill and died suddenly of a liver disease. Before he died, he pleaded with Shinyan, "Take care of Jirohachi, please take care of him."

So Shinyan took Jirohattan with him wherever he worked and treated him like a brother.

"Thanks to Jirohattan's help, the wall I plastered was praised," Shinyan always said.

"Well, Jirohattan," said the village mayor, "why don't you sing a song for Shinyan's happy departure?"

Jirohattan looked hard at Shinyan's face, then he stood up brightly. He took the towel from his waist and put it on his head, tied it under his chin and rolled up his trousers. Then he started singing a song the school children had taught him.

> Ta-a-nki, Po-o-nki, Tan-korori
> Mud snails are singing in the rice-fields.
> Ta-a-nki, Po-o-nki, Tan-korori
> Mud snails are singing a trill of a song.

Jirohattan danced, waving both hands only to the right, stamping only the left foot, to-n, to-n, to-n.

"Jirohattan, you're a good dancer!"

"Go on!" hooted several men. But as they watched him dance, they began to feel sorry for him.

"Well done, Jirohattan!" praised the policeman. But his voice sounded sad.

"Shinyan, Banzaaa-i!" cheered the mayor, standing up. But nobody joined the cheer.

The next morning, Shinyan set out early.

In front of his house a crowd of people and children carrying small flags gathered to see him off. A banner read,

MR. SHINTARO HIRANO,
CONGRATULATIONS ON GOING INTO THE ARMY!

Beneath it stood Shinyan with a red sash draped across his shoulder. The mayor started a speech to which Shinyan was supposed to reply. Then Jirohattan interrupted.

"I, too, will go! Go with Shinyan!" he said, pulling at Shinyan's sash. Jirohattan's mother rushed up and grabbed Jirohattan's hand.

"I want to go! I want to go!" Jirohattan elbowed his mother aside. She tottered as if she was going to fall down.

"Jirohachi, what are you saying!" she cried, pulling his hand. "You can't go where Shinyan is going!"

Jirohattan elbowed her again, harder than the first time. "Jirohachi! Shame on you!" Jirohattan's mother wiped her eyes with her sleeve. "For goodness sakes, persuade him, Teacher!"

I went up close to Jirohattan. "Jirohattan, don't disturb Shinyan's departure. Let's wait over there for a while." He followed me obediently.

"Wave this," I said, "and see Shinyan off nicely." I handed a small flag to him. "Let's go up to the bell tower. We'll be able to watch Shinyan going a long way from up there. Come with me."

"Teacher, where's Shinyan going?" asked Jirohattan as we walked to the bell tower.

"Shinyan is going to be a soldier and fight in the war. He's not going to plaster. When he comes back, he'll take you to work again. Let's wait for that day, okay?"

He nodded.

> We leave our country bravely,
> Swearing to win the battle.
> Let us perform this feat, or die . . .

While the children from the school sang a war song, Shinyan started off. The children followed him, waving flags with the villagers close behind.

Standing on the stone steps of the bell tower, I waved my flag. Jirohattan, too, waved his flag, and gazed at the procession that was going down the lower road far off into the distance.

21

CHAPTER 4

⋙⋘

The Straw Men

One day Jirohattan was turning over the hay that was spread out to dry on the field path. Kin came running up.

"Jirohattan! Hey, Jirohattan!" he called. "Come on! I'll show you something!" Kin took off running again.

"What is it?" asked Jirohattan.

"You'll see, just come with me. Hurry! And Kin grabbed Jirohattan, who went with scraps of hay trailing from his pants and sandals.

During the war our village was responsible for a large quota of hay for the military horses. After the grass had been mowed, we spread it outside our houses, on the field paths and anywhere outdoors. We even spread it on the rooftops, and the hay's sweet smell filled the whole village.

Mowing the grass was the schoolchildren's

homework. Early every morning they mowed through the dewy paths and then would go to school with bundles of cut grass on their backs. The playground at school was covered with drying hay.

Jirohattan helped the children mow and tie the hay into small bundles every morning. Then he would tie the bundles onto the children's backs with a straw rope. The children were really happy to mow with Jirohattan because he would do all the work for them while they played in the field.

After the hay was spread on the ground to dry, it had to be turned over to dry evenly. Without being asked, Jirohattan would go around the village in the afternoon turning over the hay wherever it was spread out.

The villagers were grateful and would say things like,

"What a wonderful help he is!"

"Each time we deliver it, we're told that our hay is the best."

"It's because of Jirohattan."

Jirohattan followed Kin to the front of Kannon Temple, a temple sacred to the goddess of mercy. It was at the edge of the village, surrounded by a grove of cedars. Two big straw men were tied with straw ropes around cedar trees in front of the small temple.

Many excited children had gathered around the straw men. "What are they?" asked Jirohattan.

"They are leaders of our enemies," Kin said.

"What?" asked Jirohattan. "Enemies?"

"Yes," said the children hitting the straw men.

"This is an American general."

"And that is an English general."

The straw men were about eight feet tall and almost one and a half arm's reach around. One had a long face and thick drooping eyebrows that looked like daggers. The other straw man had a square face with thick straight eyebrows and a pug nose. These faces were drawn on cardboard and attached to the straw at the top of the body. Each cardboard face had a battered washbowl for a hat.

"An old soldier made them," Yachan told Jirohattan.

"The sign says 'Stab them when passing by,'" said one boy. "Watch me, Jirohattan, and do as I do." He picked up a bamboo spear that leaned against one of the straw men.

"Ei-i-i!" he yelled and thrust the spear into the straw man's side. The straw bundle made the sickening sound of a stab.

"Let me do it!"

"Me too!"

"It's my turn next!"

The children dashed for the bamboo spear.

"Don't do it," said Jirohattan. "It's too sad," and he tried to take the spear away from them.

"What? Sad? They're our enemies!"

"They'll come and fight Shinyan!"

"Now, take the spear and stab Shinyan's enemies."

"No, I won't do it!" said Jirohattan.

"Ei-i-i!" he yelled and thrust the spear into
the straw man's side. The straw bundle
made the sickening sound of a stab.

"Then I'll do it for you."

The spear made a crunching sound each time it was thrust into the straw. It was an awful thing to do, even if they were only straw men.

Now I'm embarrassed at what we villagers did. But it was regarded as patriotic to hate the enemy.

"If the enemy comes, kill them with a bamboo spear," was the order we had. The women in the village were assembled together every day.

"Eii-!" "Yaa-!" We would practice jabbing with our bamboo spears. We also had a firefighting exercise, passing a pail from one person to another.

If we thought these things were foolish and didn't attend these lessons, we would be called traitors. So all of us had to do as we were told.

One day, I passed in front of the temple. Moustaches had been added to the straw men's faces.

The next day the moustaches had been changed to bushy beards and I wondered who had done it. The faces were too high for the children to reach. Then I found out that the children had done it by tying a brush smeared with ink to a pole.

With the bushy beards, the straw men's faces seemed more hateful than ever and because they'd been stabbed countless times, the straw ropes were torn off and the washbowls gone.

One morning the children found a surprise. Someone had placed flowers, Japanese roses, in a bottle in front of the straw men.

"Who would do such a thing?" the children said and kicked the bottle over.

But the next morning, roses had once more been offered to the straw men.

"Someone did it again!" the children yelled and trampled the flowers. "It must have been Jirohattan. Only he would do such a silly thing."

"It's something he would do," agreed the villagers and shouting, "Eii!," they, too, stabbed the straw men and went away.

Another day, when I happened to be passing by, Jirohattan was putting fresh flowers in the bottle. He looked at me and said, "The men are dead. It's sad, isn't it?"

The straw men's faces were torn, the straw from their bodies scattered. The cedar tree trunks showed through the remaining straw.

CHAPTER 5

୧୨୪

The Scream of the Kitah

"'Kiaah, kiaah!' Sometimes, late at night, a horrible cry screamed out over the mountains and valleys and high above the sleeping village. The people in the village said, 'It's the Kitah!' and felt terrible fear. No one knew what kind of creature made the scary sound but they believed that something awful would happen when the Kitah screamed. It almost always foretold someone's death: a man killed in an accident or a child drowned.

"During the war, the screams were heard frequently."

୧୨୪

This time Kitah's screaming had lasted two or three nights.

"How frightening! Kitah's screaming again tonight," said the villagers as they covered their ears or pulled their quilts a little tighter around themselves. The night of the Kitah dragged on.

"Will someone die soon?"

"Didn't Kitah scream when Isamu-san, the blacksmith, died at war?"

"Is someone we know going to die in battle again?" the villagers wondered anxiously. Everyone was nervous and uneasy, even in the daytime. Whenever they saw one another, the villagers talked about the Kitah and warned all the children they met to be extra careful.

"Don't play by the river or a mud turtle will grab you and pull you under the water!"

"Don't go near the pond or the Kitah will cut your liver out!"

"Kitah is a bird with a long bill."

"No, it's a beast with wings."

"It's a bird with red wings and a red bill."

Such was the whispered speculation. No one had ever seen it.

Grandma Okane came to me and announced, "A prayer will be offered at the shrine tonight. Come and pray!"

When a prayer was offered at the shrine, at least one person from every family was expected to go and pray. People said that if no one from a family went, something bad would happen to that family.

After sunset, a bonfire was lit in the shrine court. The villagers walked in a circle around the bonfire, chanting the Buddhist chant *Hannya-shingyo*.

The old man, Shunpei, who was ninety, led us. His hearing had dulled, but the scream of the Kitah was always ear-piercing, even for him.

"Maka hannya mittara shingyo . . ."

The chant rose and spread in the dark sky with the sparks of the bonfire.

Grandpa Shunpei was the wisest man in the village. So I asked him, "What is Kitah?"

"Might be a night crow," he said.

"Why is it called Kitah?"

"I don't know. It's been called that as long as I can remember."

There is an old word *kitai*, meaning mysterious. I think Kitah came from that word.

As Grandpa Shunpei said, Kitah might have been a night crow. Crows seem to know when death is near. We had a saying, "The crow cries so hard. Is the sick man going to die?"

It was nearly dawn when we went down from the mountain where we had prayed all the night. Of course, Jirohattan's mother and Shinyan's mother had prayed with us.

When Jirohattan's mother returned home, she found Jirohattan still sleeping soundly. Knowing that day would soon break, she lay down to get a little rest.

"Help! Help!" Jirohattan called out in his sleep.

Startled, his mother shook him to waken him.

"Help! Help! Help!" Jirohattan continued to cry out.

"Jirohachi, Jirohachi!" his mother said shaking him.

Jirohattan opened his eyes slightly, gasping. "Shinyan, Shinyan," he moaned and clung to his mother.

Jirohattan opened his eyes slightly, gasping. "Shinyan,
Shinyan," he moaned and clung to his mother.

"Jirohachi, what's the matter with Shinyan?" His mother shook him again, harder than before.

"Shinyan, Shinyan . . ."

"What's the matter with him? Tell me!"

"Shinyan! He drowned! Jirohattan cried and fell back on his mattress.

Then his mother had a horrible thought, "I wonder if Shinyan has been killed!"

Jirohattan slept for several days without waking up even to eat.

One month later word came that Shinyan had died.

When Shinyan joined the army, he received orders to go to an island in the Pacific Ocean. As soon as the transport ship which carried him reached the high seas, it was attacked by enemy torpedoes and sunk. All on board drowned.

Oddly enough, it happened the same day Jirohattan had the nightmare.

Shinyan's mother received a postcard from him after his death had been reported. He had written it before he left on the ship.

I am fine, so do not worry about me. I will serve our country well. Mother, take care of yourself and give my regards to everyone.

"Is this all? Is this all of my son that comes back to me?" Shinyan's mother embraced the card and shut herself up in a closet for a night and a day refusing to see those who came one after another to console her.

If word came that a soldier had died in battle, the village placed a sign above the family's front door that said, "An Honored House." They came and placed one on Shinyan's house.

"Why is this house honored?" Shinyan's mother cried to herself in the closet. "My son has been killed. How can they call it honored?

"Shintaro, you struggled and suffered, didn't you? My poor son." She talked to the postcard and wept.

Since that day, Shinyan's mother was scared of water and for a long time couldn't even take a bath.

CHAPTER 6

⁊⋆⋆⋆⋆

The Sound of the Grindstone

"When I'm sitting on these steps and listening very carefully, it seems that I can hear a faint sound.
    Rummeldidum, rummeldidum.
    It's the sound of a grindstone."

⁊⋆⋆⋆⋆

One day, Grandma Okane was grinding some barley. Sitting on the worm-eaten boards of the porch, she dropped the barley kernels one after another into the grindstone and turned the handle around and around. The stone grating on stone ground out a steady hum.

That is the sound I hear.

I can still hear her drowsy song, too.

    One, two, three, make a dream.
    Four, and five, bridge the stream.

Leaning against the bridge rail
I met a maid carrying a pail,
Flowers, incense, and fresh cream.
She had just turned eighteen.

Grandma Okane not only had the odd job of telling the news around the village, she also owned a tiny sweet-shop for children. In one corner of the earth-floor room in her house were four or five glass-covered square boxes sitting on a shelf. Flat triangle-shaped ginger sweets, long stick candy, brown-sugar candy and other cheap sweets were in these boxes. Grandma Okane lived alone and was happy to have the children as her customers.

The war dragged on and we were getting destitute. There were no sweets to be found and Grandma's boxes were empty and covered with dust. No children came around.

"I'm so lonely without the children," she thought. Then she got the idea of making barley flour with barley from her field.

While Grandma Okane was turning the grindstone, Jirohattan stopped by. "Grandma's making barley flour?" he asked.

"Ah! Jirohattan."

"Take a rest, Grandma! I'll do it!"

"No, you have the strength of a horse. If you turn the handle too hard, the flour will come out coarse and be no good."

"I'll do it slowly then."

"I'll turn the handle, but you can drop the grains in one by one when the hole comes in front of you."

"All right."

"Only drop one in. Don't do more than that."

"Okay."

"No, too much! I said one grain."

"I'm trying to drop one, but it just drops a lot."

"Your fingers are too thick. There again, too much!" Jirohattan patted his fingers and said laughing, "One by one, one by one."

Then he looked Grandma Okane in the face and said, "Grandma?"

"What?"

"When will Shinyan be back? How many nights must I sleep till he returns?"

"Shinyan? Oh dear!" Grandma Okane stopped turning the handle of the stone mill for a moment. "The poor boy," she muttered to herself.

"What?"

"Nothing, nothing. Never mind." Grandma Okane turned the handle and again the grindstone made its rumbling sound. "There, drop the barley."

"Grandma, how many nights must I sleep till Shinyan's back?"

"Let me think."

"Two?"

"No."

"Three?"

"No, more than that. He's gone far away."

"Then how many? Tell me."

"How aggravating! What awkward questions you ask."

"Aggravating? How many's that?"

"Really! Aggravated is the state I'm in. Let's say ten."

"Is this ten?" Jirohattan opened his right hand.

At that moment, they heard the sound of straw sandals coming near.

"Grandma, give me some barley flour!" Tachan dashed up.

"Just a minute, just a minute!" Grandma Okane was glad to avoid Jirohattan's questioning. She gathered the flour that had heaped under the grindstone and wrapped the tiny handful in old newspaper.

"Here," said Tachan. He handed her two wrinkly old potatoes and licked at the flour on the newspaper.

"Good, isn't it?" said Jirohattan, moving his tongue as Tachan's tongue moved.

"Delicious!" Tachan's face, his mouth powdered with flour, beamed.

Toward the end of the war, a tiny handful of barley flour was the only treat available to the children. When they heard Grandma Okane's stone grinder, they would come running. They didn't have any money so they always brought something to trade for the barley flour: a handful of barley, or rice, or a *daikon*, a Japanese radish, fresh from the field with the mud still on it.

"Tachan, how much is ten?" Jirohattan asked.

Tachan licked the newspaper completely clean, wadded it up into a ball and threw it away. "Ten?"

"Yeah."

"Ten's this much," and Tachan held up both hands, fingers spread open. Jirohattan opened his hands too, and looked at them.

"Why, Jirohattan? What's the matter?" asked Tachan.

"Grandma told me if I sleep this much, Shinyan'll be back," said Jirohattan, studying his hands and tilting his head to the side.

"Guess you're not sure how long you'll have to sleep. I'll make it easier for you," said Tachan and he told Jirohattan to tie something around each finger and when he went to bed, untie one of his fingers. When all the fingers were untied, ten days would have passed.

"Oh, Tachan! Don't teach him that. Jirohattan will take it seriously," said Grandma Okane glaring at Tachan.

Jirohattan pulled a few straws out from under the porch. "Tachan, tie my fingers with these," he said and handed the straws to Tachan.

"See, Jirohattan took it seriously. Did you have to tell him that?" scolded Grandma Okane.

Jirohattan held his hands open in Tachan's face.

"Jirohattan, it's no use," said Tachan throwing the straws down. "Shinyan died on the way to battle. He is dead. Can a man who's dead come back?"

"He'll be back!" cried Jirohattan and he made a grab for Tachan.

"If a dead man comes back, he's a g-h-o-s-t." Tachan pulled away from Jirohattan.

"He must come back! He's coming back! With fluttering flags! He's coming back! You damn boy!" Jirohattan ran after Tachan.

"The poor boy! He'll never understand," said

Jirohattan held his hands open in Tachan's face.

Grandma Okane. She dropped one grain in the hole, turned the grindstone and started to sing.

> Going up the first step, I sobbed.
> Going up the second, I wept.
> Third step, fourth step, still going up . . .

CHAPTER 7

Evacuee Children

"In 1944, towards the end of the war, a group of children from Kobe came to stay for a while in the village's temple. The arrangement was made quickly because of rumors that Kobe would soon receive serious bomb damage. These children might have been the last during the war to be evacuated from Kobe.

"Almost all the children who lived in cities had been moved to the countryside. There were two ways to evacuate to the country. One was to move the entire family into a relative's home. The other was to send only the children in a group with other children who had no relatives living in the country.

"The children who came and stayed in our temple came alone."

❧❧❧

"Many evacuee children will come today!"

Members of the Women's Society went around the village seeking mattresses and blankets for the children and rice for the welcoming party.

The Agriculture Cooperative Society brought the children from the train station to the village in trucks. The village children gathered to meet them at the edge of the village. The priest from the temple and I went too. Jirohattan came with us.

It was bitter cold. Snowflakes were drifting in the wind. Twenty-two children from the ages of eight to twelve arrived. Because they were from the city, all had beautiful fair complexions, but they looked underfed and tired.

It had been a hard trip from Kobe to the village. Evacuees were given priority on the trains but it didn't make much difference; the trains were always jammed. People climbed in and out of the windows and some who could not get in the train rode on top of the baggage cars. The city children must have been exhausted after being on the overcrowded train for so many hours.

They had air-raid hoods around their necks and a badge sewn onto their coats upon which was written the child's name, age, parent's name, address, and blood type. Each bundled-up child carried a big bag.

My heart ached for them. I decided that while they were here, I would care for them as if they were my own children. The woman who came with them was young. She looked twenty or so, the same age I was when I first came to teach in this village.

"Isn't she beautiful!" Jirohattan said, pulling my sleeve.

"How do you do?" The young woman introduced herself, "I'm Fumie Ishino, in charge of these children. Thank you for accepting us. We will be under the care of . . ." Miss Ishino, whose cheeks were red from the cold wind, could not say any more because she started to cry.

"Don't worry, Miss Ishino," said the priest. "The villagers are friendly. Rely on us." Then he patted the children on their heads and said, "Girls and boys, too, don't worry. The village children will be good friends to you soon."

"The poor children!" A murmur ran through the crowd from the Women's Society.

"I'm glad they came," Jirohattan said from behind me, wriggling his shoulders with joy.

That evening a welcoming party was given by the Women's Society, and the village children joined in.

"Rice balls are ready. Help yourselves." A big plate loaded with rice balls was offered to the children from the city. They stared amazed at the many big rice balls. No one took any.

"Now, don't hesitate," the priest said and handed a rice ball to each child. "You will have rice only tonight. From tomorrow on it will be vegetable soup."

The city children took big bites and the village children did the same. The evacuees' eyes began to shine.

"Hiroki, do you see that magnolia tree with the big, green leaves? Behind that tree can you see the old temple? That one with the ornamental railings on its roof.

"It is the temple sacred to the god of medicine. Long ago, people who were ill stayed there and prayed to be cured. The room in that temple is thirty tatami mats wide. The evacuee children stayed there. The priest called it the Kobe Villa."

❧❧❧

"Come, this is your new home." The priest led the children into the room. We made a fire in an *irori*, a hearth set into the floor in the center of the room.

"Oh! Is that an *irori*?" The children were excited because they had never seen one before. Only farmhouses had *iroris*.

To entertain the children, the women started singing a song and the children soon joined in the singing.

We kept a fire going by feeding charcoal to the glowing embers of the *irori*. It kept the room warm but charcoal was scarce. The priest had begged the village office for some charcoal for the children and had received two bags as a special ration.

That first night Jirohattan's mother stayed overnight with the children. All were tired from their long journey so they went to bed and soon were fast asleep.

Feeling a sense of relief, Jirohattan's mother slept too. Then she was awakened by the sound of sobbing. At first she thought, "It's only the wind. When the cold wind howls, it sounds as if someone is weeping."

Then she thought, "No, that couldn't be the wind. Perhaps it's the bamboo leaves rustling behind the temple.

"No, it isn't that either," she decided and rising quietly, went out onto the porch. Someone was standing under the magnolia tree. It was Miss Ishino and she was holding a child on her back.

"Miss Ishino! What are you doing out here so late? And it's so cold!" Jirohattan's mother ran to her side. Miss Ishino burst into tears and the child on her back began to sob again.

Miss Ishino explained to Jirohattan's mother that she had taken little Hisayo to the toilet. Hisayo began to cry, "Mama, Mama!" She begged to be taken home.

If the other children woke up they would start crying too, so Miss Ishino took Hisayo upon her back and stayed outside where Jirohattan's mother found her.

It was the first time Hisayo and many of the other children had slept alone. All of the children missed their parents very much. If one cried, the others would cry, too.

Hisayo slept snuggled up to Jirohattan's mother that night. From the next day on, Jirohattan's mother and I helped care for the children. She had a job as a telegraph messenger and I had housework to do, so we decided to take turns. She would come and help with the children in the morning and I would come during the day and at night. Miss Ishino was very pleased with our offer. The three of us would help each other.

Jirohattan came with his mother and was a great help to us. Every morning the children followed him to school in a double line.

"Jirohattan, what's the matter? You always take care of the city children and never play with us anymore!" Yachan, Tachan and the other village children tried to block him one morning on the way to school, but Jirohattan just grinned at them and continued on his way.

When the city children returned from school, Jirohattan took them to the mountain behind the temple to gather firewood.

"Look at me! I'm like the raccoon dog in the story of the Click Clack Mountain."

The children had fun carrying the bundles of firewood on their backs. They also worked in the empty field behind the temple, hoeing and planting potatoes and onions.

"When can we eat them?" The children were anxious about their crops and went every day to tend them.

The girls prepared the food while Jirohattan made a fire under the kitchen stove. The boys lugged buckets of water from the well to fill the bathtub and brought in bundles of firewood while Jirohattan lit a fire for the bath.

In the evening, Jirohattan made a fire in the *irori*

*Every morning the children followed
him to school in a double line.*

with the children's help. Once he managed to get some lumpy old potatoes and put those in the *irori*'s hot ashes.

> Roast potatoes, roast potatoes,
> Please roast fast!
> Who will get the first one?
> Who will get the last?

Jirohattan sang and the children sang with him until the potatoes were cooked. Then Jirohattan dug out the potatoes and, spearing them with long-handled prongs, gave one to each child. Ashes stuck to the potatoes' skin and blackened the hole made by the prongs, but to the children, the potatoes were perfectly delicious.

At night, when everyone was settled cozily around the *irori*, Jirohattan often told the story of the fox and the raccoon dog.

ᘓᘒᘓᘒᘓ

"Would you like to hear that story, Hiroki? Very well, I'll tell it to you the same way Jirohattan told it.

"A fox and a raccoon dog are like a cat and dog to each other. One day the raccoon dog decided to play a trick on the fox and turned himself into a piece of fried tofu. Well, a fox loves nothing more than fried tofu. The raccoon dog, looking like a mouth-watering piece of fried tofu, lay down on the edge of a bridge. Just then, the fox came lazily down from the mountain. 'Sniff, sniff, something smells good,' said the fox. 'Sniff, sniff,

Then Jirohattan dug out the potatoes and, spearing them with long-handled prongs, gave one to each child.

something smells sooo good.' Then he saw the fried tofu and jumped at it with a yelp.

"'Dear fox, dear fox, it's me!' called the raccoon dog as the fox fell into the water."

"At first the villagers brought pumpkins and potatoes for the children. But they soon stopped. We received less and less rationed food, and the children grew more and more hungry. Every meal they had only a little rice in watery soup.

"'Oh! Today there are some black beans in the soup!' cried one child, delighted. He tried again and again to pick them up with his chopsticks but, to his great disappointment, they were only the reflections of his eyes.

"That was one of the stories we told about the scarcity of food during the war. It described the situation well."

☙☙☙

From time to time, Jirohattan took some rice from the rice bin in his kitchen and added it to the soup for the children. His mother knew he did it and would tease him.

"Hey! The soup has turned into rice today!" she would say, or "How did so much rice appear in today's soup?"

Jirohattan would stick out his tongue and grin.

One day, two girls were crying in the corner of the temple. They told us that as they were coming back from school, they had seen a branch full of shiny ripe loquats hanging out over a fence. The loquats looked beautiful and delicious to the girls, who had never seen any before. So they stood and admired them for a little while.

Then some boys, also on their way home, came along and started to tease them.

"Oh, you're evacuees."

"Hungry evacuees, aren't you."

"Stealing loquats, huh?"

The boys then searched the girls, throwing everything out of their bags and emptying their pockets.

"We were only looking at them," the girls kept insisting. But the boys just kicked their bags.

"I want to go back to Kobe," one of the girls sobbed to us. It was hard to see them so heartbroken. Miss Ishino started to cry too.

"Don't cry any more. You two have done nothing wrong," I told them. "Wait till I get my hands on those boys. They must be from the next village to do such a wretched thing."

Jirohattan listened to what I was saying and then went out quietly. He went to the Itoya Bridge and stood there waiting for boys from the next village to cross the bridge.

"Don't be mean to the city children!" he said and whacked a boy who happened to be crossing the bridge. "You made the city girls cry!" and he hit another unlucky boy's head.

"Ouch! What'd you hit me for?"

"Hey! What did I do?"

"He's crazy!"

"Crazy Jirohattan!"

The boys started to throw stones at Jirohattan. Some village children saw what was happening and, indignant that the boys had called Jirohattan crazy, came to his defense. A rough and tumble fight broke out on the bridge between our village boys and those from the next village.

Unfortunately, even our own village children made fun of the city children at school.

"Hungry evacuees!"

"Hungry evacuees!"

Soon the city children became reluctant to go to school.

One day the fifth-grade teacher came to see the priest at the temple. A lunch box was missing from the class. One of the students claimed that it had been taken by a city child. The priest was mortified by the story. He took the six fifth-grade students before the Buddha in the main temple.

"Can you swear to Buddha, all of you, that you didn't take the lunch box?" asked the priest solemnly.

"By Buddha, I didn't take it."

"Neither did I. I never stole anything." All the children denied it.

The priest went to the school principal with the six children. "These children are under my care," he said. "I am not letting them starve or driving them to steal and eat others' lunches. Talk again to the owner of the lunch box and the student who said that one of my children had stolen it."

"We'll look into the matter some more," promised the principal and the teacher.

"I can't help it if our children are bullied by some of the other children," said the priest indignantly, "but for the teachers to be so suspicious of them is unpardonable."

A few days later, the teacher came to apologize. The missing lunch box had been left and forgotten in the playground equipment room.

The priest wished the children could bring a lunch to school, at least once, like the village children always did.

The city children only had soup to eat and weren't able to bring it to school. At noon they would run back to the temple for their soup, which was never enough. No sooner had the children returned to school than they were hungry again.

A few days after the lunch box had been found, the priest was invited to one of the villager's house to conduct a Buddhist service. After the service, it was the custom for the group to have dinner together. This time the priest made a special request.

"I'd rather have some uncooked rice than dinner today." He was pleased when they offered him three quarts of rice.

"Children, children!" the priest called as he carried the rice up the sloping path in front of the temple.

The next day, the children went to school with rice balls for lunch. The only thing included with the rice balls was some pickles, but the children were thrilled.

After that, every time the priest officiated at a Buddhist service, he wouldn't eat the dinner. Instead he would request rice for the children.

"When will the next service be?" the children would eagerly ask the priest.

One year passed since the city children had arrived in the village. That winter it snowed and snowed and snowed. At first the children were delighted and had a snowball fight in the temple yard.

But, whatever the weather, the children had to go to school, and the lonely sloping road that stretched before the temple was always deep in snow. Every wintry morning when the children set out to school, Jirohattan forged a path down the road with a snow pusher made by the priest. It was just a triangular board with a long handle.

The village children wore rubber boots to school in the snow, but the evacuee children had neither boots nor rubber shoes. Their canvas shoes were soon soaked. To try to keep their feet dry, the children put straw in their shoes, but the damp still came through and their socks were always wet.

The classroom had a heating stove which was lit with firewood each child brought to school.

"The evacuees' socks stink!" complained the village children when the wet socks were hung up to dry by the stove. So the children stopped removing their cold and wet socks and shoes at school and, as a result, their feet got frostbite. My heart ached to see them suffer so.

The priest and I asked the village office for a special ration of boots for the children. But getting twenty-two pairs of boots, of all different sizes, at one time, was impossible.

We were desperate, so we asked the Women's Society to help. In one way or another, we managed to get boots for all the children. Most were grown-ups' secondhand boots. Some were too big for the children, some had holes. But these boots were better than what they had been wearing before.

Even with the boots, the children's frostbitten hands and feet were getting worse. No medicine was available. It was terrible. "It sometimes helps to spread sap from the herb *undersnow* on the sores," said the priest.

Jirohattan heard him, stood up and went out. After clearing off the top layer of snow, he shoveled some of the bottom snow onto the towel he always wore around his waist and brought it in to the priest.

"Here's some undersnow," said Jirohattan.

"Yes, it certainly is." We laughed a lot over that.

Jirohattan's mother, who was back from delivering telegrams, said, "Applying tea made from dried *hozuki* is the best way to treat frostbite."

Hozuki tea was commonly used for children's coughs, and villagers used to hang many plants to dry in the summer shade. "Omitsu-san who lives next to the Kannon Temple might have some," Jirohattan's mother said. "Jirohachi, go and ask her for it. The dried *hozuki*, do you understand?"

"The dried *hozuki*, the dried *hozuki*," Jirohattan repeated.

"That's right. Go ask for it," his mother said. "If she says she has some, then you ask, 'Please let me have some of it.'"

Jirohattan went out repeating *hozuki* over and over again. At dusk, snowflakes began to flutter.

It was dark and Jirohattan was still not back. "Where's he gone?" We were getting worried about him.

Finally, covered with snow, he came back crying. "Nobody had it! I got none!"

He had gone from house to house all over the village asking for *hozuki*. But no one had any.

Four or five days after that, Jirohattan came to the temple carrying a big bundle wrapped in a large cloth. It held many dried *daikon* leaves. Sankichi-san, a *tatami* mat maker had given them to him telling him to "Make the children's sore feet warm with this."

We were very thankful for it. Immediately we filled a large kettle with as many leaves as we could and boiled them. When they had simmered enough, the color of the boiling water had turned brown.

So as not to waste the boiled leaves, we put them aside in a bamboo basket. Two at a time, the children put their sore feet into a washtub that was filled with warm *daikon* tea. Slowly we added hotter and hotter tea.

"Who's next?"

"It's your turn."

All the children went through the experiment. A bath with *daikon* leaves added to the water was supposed to be good for the circulation.

And how do you think the boiled leaves were used? We chopped them up, fried them in oil, and the children ate them all.

That spring, to our great dismay, the city children became flea-ridden. Since we had no soap, it was impossible to remove all the dirt from their clothes. Even when we poured hot water on the clothes, we were unable to get rid of the fleas.

At school the city children were teased. "The evacuees are full of fleas! Don't go near them or you'll get their fleas!"

Miss Ishino, Jirohattan's mother and I discussed what to do and decided to boil all of the flea-ridden clothes. We set a big kettle on stones next to the bell tower, filled it with water and lit a bonfire under it. This was one of Jirohattan's tasks. He kept the fire blazing under the kettle while the clothes boiled. Then he took the boiled clothes down to the Okawa River and gave them a good washing.

Jirohattan was happy to go to the river to wash the clothes because Miss Ishino always went with him. If it was a beautiful day, they would spread out all the washed clothes on the river bank in the morning and return to fetch the dried clothes in the evening.

If it was rainy, Jirohattan complained all day, "We can't go to the river to wash today," and wiped his nose.

On the fifteenth of August, 1945, the war ended.

All the people in the village heard His Majesty the Emperor's announcement over the radio and cried bitterly over the defeat of Japan.

But the evacuee children were full of joy.

"Now we can go back to Kobe!"

"We can go home!"

Some of the children immediately began to gather their belongings.

"Wonderful!" I said, feeling the children's great joy. "You're all safe and able to return to your families."

Jirohattan came in and saw the children's preparations.

"Why are you packing your things?" he asked.

"We are going back to Kobe."

"Why are you going back there?"

"The war has ended!"

Jirohattan watched the happy children. "Really, are you going away?" he asked, cocking his head to one side.

"Stay a little longer and I'll go swimming with you in the river. It's fun," he tried to persuade them. My heart ached for Jirohattan as he talked to the busy children while they rushed around preparing to leave. Looking after these children had been a great pleasure for him.

A farewell party was given the last evening the children were with us. Parting, even a joyful parting, is sad. The children had stayed here only a little over a year, but all of us had many unforgettable memories.

The Women's Society collected a donation of rice from the village again and made a lunch for the children to take with them. Two big rice balls, wrapped in bamboo leaves, were given to each child.

Miss Ishino took Jirohattan's hand and said, "Thank you so much for everything! I shall never forget all you've done for us. I only have this as a present to give you." She gave him her pen engraved with her name, Fumie Ishino.

The next day, Miss Ishino and the children set off. They were taken to the train station by the same trucks that had brought them. Jirohattan stood, crying, on a stone step at the bell tower and watched them leave.

"Jirohattaa-n!"

All the children called his name aloud, standing up in the moving trucks and looking toward the temple.

The children's calls were heard till the trucks had turned the corner of the mountain.

"Jirohattaa-n!"

"Jirohattaa-n!"

CHAPTER 8

Reminders

"After Miss Ishino and the children had returned to Kobe, Jirohattan became moody. He seemed to be in a daze and idled his time away just sitting by the temple's irori *or on these stone steps, staring at the blackened earth where the big iron cauldron had been set to boil the evacuee children's flea-ridden clothes.*

"He always kept with him the picture book Taro Urashima *and the pen Miss Ishino had given him."*

One evening towards dusk, a cicada chirped noisily on the pine tree's branch by the temple gate while Jirohattan sat on the stone steps.

"Jirohattan!" I called to him. He gave me a sad look. "Do you have the picture book?"

"Uh huh," he said and handed it to me.

Pretending I was reading it, I looked at him out

of the corner of my eye and turned the pages to the picture of the palace. He patted my hand and said, "Teacher, read it to me. Read it from the first page."

I started to read, "Once upon a time, in a seaside village, there lived a young fisherman whose name was Taro Urashima . . ."

Jirohattan interrupted when I started reading about the sea princess.

"This sea princess and Miss Ishino look alike, don't they?" he said.

"Yes, they do," I said. "If Miss Ishino were wearing this beautiful kimono, she'd look like a sea princess." Jirohattan drew nearer to me.

"Where can we buy this kimono?" he asked me and took out his purse, which he kept hung around his neck.

"Well, no shops have it. The sea princess wears the finest kimono at the palace and one can only find a kimono like it there," I said.

"Oh," he said, disappointed.

The next day, Jirohattan rushed up to me, "Teacher, Teacher!" He held out three letters. "Here, read them for me!"

One was from Miss Ishino. The other two were from evacuee children, Noriko Hama and Keiji Yamauchi.

"Let me see them," I said and took the letters. "Which one shall I read first?"

"The one from Miss Ishino!" Jirohattan said eagerly.

Dear Jirohattan,

How are you?

Thank you so much for all the care you gave to us. After I returned to Kobe, I started teaching again.

Whenever I tell my class a story, it is always about you. And whenever I see one of the children I took to your village, we start talking about you!

Jirohattan, I hope you are well and as happy as ever. I will come and see you some time. It is the only way I can think of to thank you.

Please give my best wishes to your mother.

Take care of yourself.

> Sayonara,
> Fumie Ishino

"This is from Keiji Yamauchi," I said and read,

Dear Jirohattan,

How are you doing? Thank you for taking care of me while I was in your village.

Many parts of Kobe were badly damaged by bombs. We were fortunate. My house, school and friends are all safe.

I go to school every day. Jirohattan, what are you doing now?

I told my class the story about the fox and the raccoon dog that you told us. They liked it and said it was funny and that they would like to meet you.

I also told my class about the snow and how we played. They said they want to visit your village. I hope you can read my letter. Ask your mother to read it for you.

> Sayonara,
> Keiji Yamauchi

"This last one is from Noriko Hama."

Dear Jirohattan,
How are you? And how is your mother?
I often see my friends who went to your village
with me. We always ask each other, "I wonder how
Jirohattan is doing?" Being away from home was
hard, but all my friends envy my stay in the
mountain village. I've told them a lot about it. I
hated it when we were accused of things we hadn't
done and when the boys were mean to us. But it was
nice that you went to fight for us.
My mother wants to meet you.
Come with your mother and visit me in Kobe.
We were very lucky that our house had no damage.

Sayonara,
Noriko Hama

"Jirohattan, you must be so happy!" I said and
turned to look at him. His eyes were filled with
tears.

One afternoon, a few days later, I stopped by
Jirohattan's house. I could hear a child's voice
coming from inside the house. "Write straight
down like this and turn it here with a swish," said
the voice. "This is the letter 'shi.' It's easy isn't it, like
a fishhook. Now, write it with your finger. Straight
down. That's it. There swish up to the right. Good!
Good!"

Someone was teaching Jirohattan how to write.
The voice sounded like Kin's and I left, letting them
continue their work.

The next morning, I stopped by again.

63

Jirohattan was writing at the low table by the window, and many papers were scattered about.

"Jirohattan," I asked, "are you studying?"

"Oh, Teacher, come in!" His voice sounded cheerful. He had written "shi" and "n," many times. "Your writing is very good!" I said.

"Kin taught me." He was all smiles.

"He was so happy to get the letters from Miss Ishino and the children," said Jirohattan's mother, "he's decided to write a letter too, first of all to Shinyan. Jirohachi asked Kin if he wrote a letter to Shinyan, would he come back? Kin said he would. He didn't dare say no."

It took many days, but Jirohattan learned to write "Shinyan." He handed his mother the paper he had written "Shinyan" on and asked her to put it into an envelope and send it to Shinyan.

"Why doesn't Shinyan come back?" Jirohattan kept pestering his mother. "I wrote to him. I wrote to him with the pen Miss Ishino gave me."

Jirohattan's mother didn't know what to say and went to the priest for advice. He had no idea and came to talk with me. I was at a loss for an answer too. It seemed cruel to lead Jirohattan on, waiting so earnestly for someone who could never return. How could we make him understand that Shinyan was dead and would never come back?

Many days passed and Jirohattan's mother, the priest and I could not find an answer. "How should we tell him?" I thought about it all the time.

One night while taking a bath, soaking snugly shoulder deep in the tub, I found myself singing a little song.

> Long, long ago, far under the sea
> Taro held tight to the turtle's black shell
> And off they went to the undersea realm.
> No picture can describe its beauty.

Then an idea came to me.

"I know! I'll tell him a story with the help of the picture book *Taro Urashima*."

The next morning, I went to see Jirohattan. I looked in at the back door. Jirohattan was writing at the low wooden table and his mother was standing by watching him.

"Good morning," I called. "Is Jirohattan studying again?"

"Yes!" he answered beaming.

"He wants to write to Miss Ishino this time," Jirohattan's mother said, "and is learning to write 'Ishino.'"

"Miss Ishino is coming back, too," he said happily. "Jirohattan," I said, "Show me your picture book about Taro Urashima."

He brought it out from under the table and handed it to me. I opened it to the picture of the sea princess and Jirohattan studied it.

"How beautiful the palace is!" I began. "And the sea princess is a real beauty, too. Her beauty grows each time I look at her." Jirohattan grinned.

"Shinyan's lucky," I said, "to be living with such a beautiful sea princess in a gorgeous palace." Jirohattan looked at me startled. I repeated it again. "Don't you think Shinyan must be very happy living with the lovely princess in a palace?"

Jirohattan stared hard into my eyes and questioned me. "Is Shinyan in the palace? With the sea princess?"

"Yes, he is."

"Why?"

"Shinyan was taken far away," I told him, "by the ship that was going to war. It sailed on a wide, wide sea. But the ship was sunk by an enemy's torpedo, which is the devil's invention. It sank with many soldiers on it. Shinyan, too, went down to the bottom of the sea.

"But Jirohattan, the palace is at the bottom of the sea and Shinyan went to live there. Look at what a gorgeous palace it is!" I pointed to the book. "Now he is with the beautiful sea princess. He can not come back to us. The palace is too far away."

Jirohattan peered into my eyes. I had nowhere else to look so we stared at each other. I felt it was a very long stare.

I continued with a choking feeling.

"Jirohattan, you haven't seen the sea yet. Let's go to the sea where Shinyan is." I was astonished at what I had said because I had not thought of it before. Tears fell down my cheeks.

"Yes, I'll go," he nodded.

I asked Jirohattan's mother to give me all the letters that Jirohattan had written to Shinyan and left. I could hear Jirohattan saying to his mother, "Mama, Shinyan won't be coming back. And I'm going to the sea."

CHAPTER 9

ชวฺชวฺ

Sending Leaf Boats

I wrote to Miss Ishino and told her that Jirohattan was learning to write with the pen she had given him. He had learned how to write "Shinyan" and was working on learning to write "Ishino." I told her about my promise to take Jirohattan to the sea and so on.

Miss Ishino wrote back quickly. "I am very thankful to Jirohattan for having helped me so much. I wish I could do something for him. Let me join you on your trip to the sea."

Both Jirohattan's mother and the priest liked my idea of taking Jirohattan to the sea. We discussed the date. Since the cold would soon be coming to Tajima, we decided to go as soon as possible, the beginning of October.

Again I wrote to Miss Ishino and she replied, "I will take some days off from work and come with you." All of us looked forward to seeing her.

I thought carefully about the best way to send Jirohattan's letters to Shinyan. To send out only the paper onto the water wouldn't be good because it would soon sink. I decided to use the magnolia leaf. The priest had once told me that the magnolia was the memorial tree of Shinyan's birth.

When Shinyan was born, his father planted a magnolia tree to show his delight at the birth of a son. The tree had grown very big. During the rainy season, big, thick, white flowers bloomed. Their fragrance was wonderful.

I made ten leaf boats, each with a letter tied to the stalk and ten more with a letter sewn inside the leaf boat. I kept the twenty leaf boats secret.

"Jirohattan, today an earthly princess is coming!" I told him that morning. "Have your hair cut and get a shave from the barber."

Dusk came early in the autumn at Tajima and it was already dark when Miss Ishino arrived. We had not seen her for almost two months and during that time she had regained some weight and had become prettier.

"Jirohattan," I called to him, "Miss Ishino is here and wants to see you." But he was too shy to come close.

That night, Jirohattan built a fire in the *irori* at Yakushi Temple and roasted potatoes as Miss Ishino had requested.

"I feel as if the children were here," she said and stroked the drawings on the wall that the children had made.

"Jirohachi," said his mother, "show Miss Ishino

the picture of the sea princess in your book. He says it looks just like you and admires it every day." Jirohattan tucked his head into his shoulders like a turtle and stirred the ashes in the *irori*.

The next morning, Jirohattan rose before the sun. He put on his new shoes and sat on the porch until we were ready to go. Jirohattan's mother had managed to get the new shoes from the city.

Our plans were to take a train from the Yabu station on the Sanin line. Yabu is the station I arrived at the first time I came to the village, about four miles away.

The four of us, Jirohattan, Miss Ishino, Jirohattan's mother and I, headed the way the morning dew had fallen, excited like little children on an excursion. We took the train the direction of Yoka - Ebara - Toyooka - Genbudo - Kinosaki - Takeno and got off at Kasumi, known for its beautiful sea and rock-strewn beach.

The sea was calm and because it was autumn, the beach was empty. Each time a large wave dashed against the rocks, the white foam rose up with a splash.

"Jirohattan," I said, "this is the sea." He looked out at his first view of the ocean in open-eyed wonder.

Jirohattan pointed to the horizon and asked, "Till there, all is the sea?" Watching a ship in the distance, he asked, "What's that?" He was curious about everything.

I explained to a fisherman why we had come and asked if he would take us out in his boat. He kindly agreed.

"I'm scared!" Jirohattan shook all over and getting him into the boat took a lot of effort. He clung tightly to the side of the boat when it set sail.

Our boat sailed between sheer rocks. "Look into the sea," said the fisherman, turning to us. "You can see the fish." The sea was a clear blue. Many fish were swimming together and it was like looking into a huge aquarium. Jirohattan gazed into the sea, clutching the side of the boat.

"Jirohachi, look at all the fish," said his mother, holding onto his back. "There's a picture like this in your book, isn't there?"

I asked the fisherman to stop the boat where there were no more rocks and I took the leaf boats wrapped in paper from my bag. "Jirohattan, these are the letters you wrote to Shinyan. Send them to him." I handed one to him.

Both Miss Ishino and Jirohattan's mother were impressed by my leaf boats. "Wonderful!" Miss Ishino said admiringly.

"Now," I told Jirohattan, "put the boat on the water and wish it to go to Shinyan." Jirohattan set the leaf boat floating on the sea.

"Oh! It's a magnolia leaf!" Jirohattan's mother stared at it. "Shinyan," she said, leaning over the side of the boat with tears in her eyes, "it's a leaf from the magnolia tree that the priest used to scold you and Jirohachi for climbing."

"Call his name," Jirohattan's mother said to him, taking the leaf boats from me and handing them to him. "Say 'Hellooo Shin-yaa-n!' Say, 'Shin-yaa-n, it's me!' Call him!"

I prayed for something, I knew not what, to direct the leaf boats set to the mercy of the waves. Miss Ishino seemed to be feeling as I was. She watched Jirohattan's hand put the leaf boats down upon the waves.

All twenty boats were at last floating on the sea. A seagull flew up over the leaf boats. Some were floating apart, some were gathered together.

Holding tightly onto the side of the boat, Jirohattan bent forward to the sea and said, "Shinyan, stay there. I'll come and visit you again."

CHAPTER 10

ﾟﾟﾟﾟ

Higan Blossoms

"Hiroki, you've been a good listener though my story has been long. You asked to know what became of Jirohattan. Okay, I'll tell you."

ﾟﾟﾟﾟ

After returning from the sea, Jirohattan became the priest's helper, sweeping all around the temple, running errands, going with the priest when he called on the villagers and things like that. He was healthy and strong and worked hard every day.

"Jirohachi, take a rest," sometimes the priest would tell him. Then he would come and sit here on this stone step of the bell tower.

On September 25, 1950, at sunrise, Jirohattan died. He died quickly and unexpectedly. "Heart attack," said the doctor.

"Mama, so many flowers are blooming." The

evening before he died he had come home with an armful of flaming red wild higan blossoms he had gathered from behind the temple.

"Mama, I'm going to study now." He wrote "Ishino" many times. Later he folded his papers neatly and put them on the low table. "Mama, I'm finished."

"Mama, have some *manju*." Jirohattan and his mother ate some rice cakes that the priest had given to him at the temple that day. "These are good," he said and went happily to bed.

He never woke up again.

Miss Ishino and two children representing all the evacuee children came to the funeral, bringing a beautiful wreath with them. One of the children read a letter in appreciation of Jirohattan. Everyone cried.

Many villagers and children joined the funeral procession from Jirohattan's house. Jirohattan's mother remained by herself and saw him off from the front door. Because of tradition, she couldn't go with Jirohattan's funeral procession.

The procession went up the red clay path to the graveyard. A paper lantern tied to the top of a bamboo tree made a rustling sound as it swung and jostled the bamboo leaves. On the lantern was written:

Name: Jirohachi Yamane
Age: Thirty-eight

The bell that Grandma Okane rang echoed

hollowly through the valley below.

Jirohattan was laid in a red clay grave while the priest chanted a prayer. Many higan blossoms were thrown onto the coffin by the children who had gathered them along the way. Bit by bit, the red flowers were covered with red earth.

"Jirohattan, have a good journey into the world beyond. Shinyan's waiting for you," Grandma Okane said and rang the bell more loudly. Of course his picture book and his pen were laid with him.

Postscript

After the Second World War, Japan became an industrialized, Westernized country in a very short time. The setting of Jirohattan *is wartime, but the lives of the people described in the story are rooted in a culture in which agriculture predominated for over two thousand years, a time when many folktales originated.*

In Japanese folktales the central characters are often grandfathers and grandmothers. These old people show the wisdom that is considered essential for coping with hardship. In Jirohattan, *the grandmother's telling of the story enables her grandson to understand what people's lives were like during the war and to appreciate what Jirohattan contributed to their lives.*

Because the tale of Taro Urashima is one of the most popular folktales in Japan, it was not necessary for Hana Mori to mention its ending in Jirohattan, *but Western readers may be interested: After staying at the palace for three years, Taro wants to go back. The princess hands him a small box, instructing him to open it when he has lost all hope. In his home village, he knows no one, and his house is no longer there, since three hundred years have passed while he was away. In despair, Taro opens the box; a waft of smoke rises from it. Suddenly, his face becomes wrinkled, his hair turns white, he bends with age, and is dead in an instant.*

Taro, a typical character in Japanese literature, is not adventurous, and does not marry the princess, but accepts whatever happens in his life. In that respect, Taro and Jirohattan resemble each other.